MOB LIFE IN THE HOOD

M. E. PERRY

ISBN: 979-8-9891687-1-2

A grim look into the life of a young hustler who propels himself into the hierarchy of organized crime.

A gritty tale of crime, violence, and betrayal.

A high-tension ride into the daily life of a low-level hoodlum rising to syndicate associate.

MOB LIFE IN THE HOOD

THE STORY OF A YOUNG HUSTLER RISING UP INTO THE FAST-PACED, VIOLENT WORLD OF ORGANIZED CRIME.

Dedication

In loving memory of Elaine Mitchell

Table of Contents

Prologue

Josh is a smart young kid growing up in the heart of the South Bronx during the sixties who comes to terms with his innate ability to relate to and manipulate people to his own ends. Born to hard-working catholic parents but enticed by the exciting and lucrative life of organized crime. He quickly finds out that getting out is a lot harder than getting in.

CHAPTER ONE

Introduction

What a farce. Me standing here in my new, well-fitted blue suit, clean-shaven, and accompanying my bright blue eyes with the kindest, most innocuous expression. My mother was in a sun dress that I had never seen before, with tears in her eyes. I was braced for the worst, despite the sunny disposition of my high-priced lawyer, who was paid for with a second mortgage on a house my father fully paid off 15 years ago. After much debate, his will was broken by my mother's insistence. It literally killed him to do it. Now, we both have to live with the guilt. Despite all of their sacrifices, all I cared about at this point was myself. Who am I kidding? My own safety and well-being were paramount to me above anyone or anything my entire life. I chose a trial by judge over a jury, especially after hearing the sentences handed out to my cohorts. Self-preservation and my slimy lawyer convinced me to separate myself from them in this legal battle. I was portrayed as the good kid led astray by a bad crowd. Little did anyone other than my father know that when it came to criminality, I was always the leader of the pack.

Being born a frail white kid in the heart of the South Bronx in the early 60s, I can tell you that my daily life was no walk in the park. The only thing that kept me alive to this point was my uncanny ability to form alliances with the most disagreeable people. My parents had good civil service jobs and were more than able to join the rest of our neighbors in white flight. But my father thought it made no sense that so many white families fled the neighborhood when black and brown families started moving in, placing themselves under financial strain and paying twice the rent for neighborhoods that were no better or safer. He was determined to stay where we were and save enough money to buy a house for the family.

My mother, Mary Gould, was a dutiful wife and pretty much went along with most of the decisions my father made. But don't get me wrong, on the rare occasions when she disagreed with him, she usually got her way. He'd put up a good fight but eventually deferred to her opinion. She was a gentle woman with nerves of steel. Although I've seen her angry on many occasions, I never heard her raise her voice in anger. When angered, she would go into a state of deep contemplation, thinking carefully about what appropriate words and actions were necessary to successfully solve the issue. My father, John, was a firm yet gentle man who had the look of a vicious mobster but the temperament of a priest. He fought with honor in the Korean War and returned as a decorated hero. After returning from the war, he got a job as a bricklayer for the city and settled into this neighborhood. They both thought that It was a quiet and safe place to raise a kid, and it was. When the first wave of troops was sent to Vietnam in 65, things started to slowly change. The first wave of casualties and soldiers who had completed their tours began returning, and cities all over the country (which were the most prominent make-up of the returning soldiers) were plagued with drugs and unrest. Inflation was high, and so was racial tension all across the country with the onset of the civil rights movement. Gang activity increased, and things were taking a downward turn in the neighborhood. It was still reasonably safe. Most of the crimes were petty theft, and violence was limited between gang members.

CHAPTER TWO

Into The Life

My parents spent many days in the principal's and dean's office, summoned there because of something I did or didn't do. At first, it was just for minor scuffles with other students while defending myself or my best friend from bullies. My body wasn't impressive enough to ward off bullies, but my father taught me early in life to always stand up for myself. He told me that by fighting for my rights, people would respect me, even if I lost the fight. He always used the civil rights activist as the prime example of what he was saying. "No matter what indignities they have to endure, they just keep on fighting; they can't lose because they won't give up." Later, as I became more well-known, I had little to no problems with bullies. It's not that anyone was afraid of me, but they knew I wouldn't give up, and it became too much of a hassle for them to start anything with me. There was a running joke told by many in my school and neighborhood. “Fighting with Josh is a no-win scenario. You would be laughed at for beating up a lanky white kid or chastised for being beaten up by a lanky white kid; either way, you’ll end up with just as many scrapes and bruises”. My new social position made me more confident and bolder. Unfortunately, arrogance and insolence came along with the package.

The first real trouble I got into was at the age of twelve. Me and my best bud, Cliff, loved gangster movies and role-played on many occasions. One day, we saw a woman removing groceries from her car and taking them into her house; we noticed that she left her purse in the front seat with the door open as she made her many trips back and forth. It only took two trips before we had her timed out, and I moved in quickly to snatch the purse. Her husband must’ve been watching through a window because he was out like a flash the minute I had the purse in my hands. Cliff and I took flight in different directions; the husband followed me since I was the one with the goods. He came close to catching me at one point, but he tripped and slammed his head into the concrete pavement. I remember finding it hilarious how hard he hit the ground, never thinking once about the possible injury or even death he could have incurred. Cliff and I later met at our planned rendezvous spot and divvied up the cash after dumping the purse in a trash can. Later in my life, I thought back on the incident and shuddered at the amount of money in credit cards or other valuables that could've been inside that purse.

The husband had to be rushed to the hospital with a fractured skull, and the cops were all over our neighborhood looking for suspects. The crime was well out of our neighborhood, but the cops knew that the culprits weren't from the area where the crime occurred. After a couple of weeks, I was picked up by the cops for questioning because I fit the description of the suspect. The victim's husband was out of the hospital and on the mend, so they brought him into the station to identify me or one of the other suspects in a lineup. It was a stroke of luck for me that the cops actually did a good job lining up people who “fit the description.” Although he identified me as the one he was chasing, he admitted he wasn’t 100% sure because three of us in the lineup looked similar enough to be brothers. The cops were convinced it was me from all they had uncovered in their investigations, but the prosecutor wouldn’t bring charges under those present circumstances. The cops made sure to let me know that they knew it was me and vowed to keep a very close eye on me. They even alerted my parents of their findings. My mother thought I was innocent, and she was just happy that I wasn’t going to jail. My father wasn’t sure but leaned towards my guilt. He never looked at me the same after that day. That might’ve been because of my lack of empathy when the cops told them that the victim’s husband could’ve died if he didn’t get care as fast as he did.

By the age of seventeen, I had already dropped out of school and was well on my way to a glorious career in crime. My innate gift of creating alliances helped me form my first crew. I wanted my best bud Cliff to be my right-hand man since he was the only person that I trusted completely, but he was so rattled by that first purse heist we pulled off that he vowed never again to put himself in a position that would jeopardize his freedom. I couldn't get him to be an active member of the crew, but he vowed to guide me through some of the more intricate dynamics of dealing with the local gangs. In essence, he became the crew's consigliere.

CHAPTER THREE

A Big Step Up

We didn't give our crew an official name, but we fashioned it after all the mob movies I watched. I started referring to it as "Our Thing." We were cautious not to use it around anyone outside the crew, fearing that some real wise guy or connected mobster would take offense and put us in a world of hurt. The crew liked it, and it stuck.

Our main activity was petty crimes, burglaries, and smash-and-grab jobs from closed businesses and cars during the night. We were smart enough to plan every heist, and as long as no one was hurt, the cops showed little interest in making us a priority. They just filled out their reports, filed them, and went on with their daily business of earning revenue for the city from working slobs who parked in the wrong spot or were caught going a couple of miles over the speed limit. That's when they weren't harassing poor neighborhood kids for loitering, drinking in public, or subway hopping. After a few years of success, we expanded the business to include weed but swore not to get involved with the substances that cops tended to make their investigative priority. Doing so would've brought in more money but would've heightened the risk of exposure and lengthy prison sentences. At first, we only sold small amounts to well-established customers, but our revenue started to swell so large that we caught the eye of a much larger criminal group who wanted a cut of the money we were bringing in, putting us in danger of losing it all. With the help of my silver tongue, I was able to make a deal that essentially gave them control of our entire operation but allowed us to be a part of their organization as minor associates. It may not sound like such a brilliant move, but it gave us less risk and more money by allowing us to expand into some of their territory. I was still able to keep command and control of my crew, but my operational guidelines came from their business manager.

We became distributors and transferred bulk amounts to different crews throughout The Bronx. During that time, we continued our smash-and-grab operation at night. I expanded my crew and separated them into day and night shifts, keeping them separated from each other.

The Organization didn't have a problem with what we were doing at night but warned me of severe consequences if I endangered their operation by mixing businesses while on their clock. Since I had to sleep like everyone else, I put one of my guys in charge of the night crew. Darren was a bit of a loose cannon, but he was smart and loved the money he was making too much to fuck it up with some reckless act or to let anyone else fuck it up for him. I could trust him with the night crew, but he was a bit too unpredictable to get involved with the organization's business. Darren was the cousin of my best bud, Cliff. He had been lobbying Cliff for months for an introduction, but Cliff refused. He decided to take it upon himself to apply for a spot in our thing. He came clean from the start about his cousin not wanting to introduce him to me, and his honesty made me believe he was worth a look at. Then again, it might've just been his cunning way of ingratiating himself to me. I knew he was Cliff's cousin because I met him once before, and he undoubtedly knew I would check with Cliff before even considering him. Cliff was still giving us advice and information but was more low-key about it after we joined the organization. He wanted no part of them. Cliff told me precisely what my keen sense of sizing up people told me. He said Darren was smart, loyal, and tough as nails. His only character flaws were arrogance and unpredictability.

I believed that those traits would be more of a benefit than a disadvantage to our crew, and I needed someone who could keep the guys in the night crew in line. With a newly elected Mayor, the cops were starting to get a little more proactive in combating crimes in the city, and one slip-up could sink the entire night operation. Darren was very aggressive in getting things done. He was five feet, ten inches of solid muscle, and had an uncanny attention to detail. He was someone who could run a top-tier Fortune Five-Hundred company like a Swiss watch and moonlight as a mob enforcer. He had all the attributes needed for success in any business. I was not surprised when he told me he had met with a rep. from the organization and applied for a position outside of our crew. Once again, he was covering his bases by letting me know that he went behind my back, just like he had done with Cliff when seeking a spot in our thing. I gave them the same information Cliff had given to me about Darren. The Organization's business manager was a distinguished-looking man whom I believed was a lawyer; at least he looked like one. Everyone called him Mr. Walker, so I addressed him in the same manner on the few occasions I had interacted with him. Seeing him was usually a sign that something important was in the works, good or bad. He was keeping an eye on our night crew's operation and had planned on approaching Darren for a position; Darren just beat him to the punch. I had no choice but to accept the organization's decision. Luckily, I had my number one on the day crew to take over for Darren; this increased my workload because, at this point, I was more managerial than hands-on. Theresa (Terry) was handling all the road work and the day crew for the last year. Initially, her only job was keeping track of the money, but she quickly expanded her duties well beyond that, and I was glad of it. She was like a Darren without the muscles or attitude. Terry was a member of the organization long before we came on the scene; their manager assured me it was the best move for all when he made the introduction. Having their own member keeping track of the money kept the heat off us if the count came up short for any reason. I got permission to switch Terry onto the night crew for the low cost of twenty percent of the operation. I didn't delude myself; the organization was slowly taking control of everything, but we were still making more money than we could've ever made without them. They also provided protection from other small gangs and had lawyers and a few cops on the payroll. They replaced her on the day crew with a shady kid named Jacan, who was not much older than me. His shifty eyes and deceptive behavior gave me great concern. That concern was amplified when I found out he was the brother of one of the high-ranking members. My keen ability to size up people told me this guy was a train wreck looking for a place to happen.

CHAPTER FOUR

A Rat In The Ranks

It didn't take long for Jacan to confirm my suspicions. He told me there was a big problem with one of the crews we supplied and insisted that I go along with him on the next delivery to straighten it out. This was a big departure from our usual method of sending two of the crew members. Everything about it seemed wrong, and I was not about to be caught up in some mess he may have concocted, so I immediately informed Mr. Walker about the situation. After letting me know that he was unaware of any of it, and checking with higher-ups, He gave me the go-ahead and told me to be cautious. This situation was getting more bizarre by the minute, but I had little choice but to follow their instructions. Jacan drove us to a warehouse on the outskirts of town, it was a place that we had used many times in the past for transactions with dealers and distributors. I believed it was owned by the organization because it was always vacant unless we were using it. Jacan had this smug look of satisfaction on his face as he parked nearly fifty yards from the nearest thing that resembled a door. No sooner than we exited the vehicle we were blocked in by three cars screeching to a stop all around us. I immediately thought that Jacan had set me up with the cops in order to take over the crew, or maybe it was the organization's last move to do just that. But it didn't make sense. Not only was I a big earner for the organization, they could've sent me packing at any time without fuss or drama, and they knew that. I kept my hands high and in sight as I leaned back on the car. Things came to light when a half dozen armed gang members in ski masks that only exposed their eyes and mouths exited the first two cars and went directly for the package in Jacan's hands. He never said a word or put up any resistance. This charade was so transparent it was shameful. The guy taking the package even smiled at Jacan right out in the open. He then moved close to me and pressed the muzzle of the gun to my forehead. No words were exchanged;

I took it as a clear signal telling me to keep my mouth shut. They got back into the two cars and rode off. The windows were tinted, but I got a good look at one of them through the windshield of the third car that no one had gotten out of. Jacan told me that I didn't have to do anything and that he would make a report to Mr. Walker. This fool actually tried to convince me that this was a thing that "Happened once in a while" and that it was just the price of doing business. I had to choke back my laughter.

I've had this operation going for nearly five years without incident, and in less than two weeks with this Buffoon, I get my first robbery after letting him change our well-thought-out routine.

Just when I thought the situation couldn't get any more ridiculous, the word on the street was that Jacan was spreading innuendos that I was somehow responsible for the robbery. I never told the business manager I believed Jacan set the whole thing up. I didn't want to implicate a family member of one of the higher-ranking members without concrete proof, but after hearing this childish clown was trying to put the blame on me, I felt I had no choice but to do something. After calling Mr. Walker and telling him that I needed to speak with him about an urgent matter, he told me that he believed he knew what I wanted to talk about, but it would have to wait. Before I could make a second request, Mr. Walker assured me that everything was being handled and he would call me in a couple of days. It was clear that he knew exactly what I was concerned about, but it wasn't clear if they believed that I was the root of the problem. After all, it was the word of a short-time low associate over one of their own. Although they all knew Jacan was a complete mess, he was also family.

CHAPTER FIVE

A Rude Awakening

As promised, Mr. Walker got back in touch with me two days later and asked me to meet him at the same warehouse where Jacan and I were robbed. I couldn't read his voice, which was unusual for me. That was the day that I realized that when facing what I thought was a life-or-death situation, I lost the bulk of my perceived superpower. This was the first time in my life that I experienced great self-doubt. Darren was sent to pick me up and transport me to the location. He was dressed better than usual and driving a non-descript car that was as much out of his character as his new attire. His demeanor was grave, but I didn't sense any danger from him. My superpower was now telling me to relax, but after that earlier moment of doubt, I couldn't completely trust it.

We rolled up to the front of the warehouse, but this time, Darren parked the car close to the structure adjacent to the large steel door.

Darren let out a heavy sigh and said, "Let's get this over with." Even with that ominous sigh and those foreboding words, I didn't feel any danger; this time, I trusted my feelings with only a bit of apprehension. I jumped out of the car like I was going to a party. I realized that not only was I innocent (Lol! well, innocent of any action against the organization), I was a lot smarter than Jacan and more trusted. When Darren pushed open the large steel door, it looked like I wasn't too far off about a party being held behind them. Mr. Walker was front and center, he turned to face me with a grim stare. There were several organization members that I'd never seen before, nearly a dozen crew members from both shifts, and Terry stood petrified with teary eyes and a terrified look on her face. As Darren and I moved in closer, the crowd parted, and there was Jacan. He was literally crucified to the back wall of the warehouse along with three other men. I recognized one of them as the guy I got a glance of through the windshield of one of the robbery cars. They were all beaten to a bloody pulp. Jacan was the only one who showed any sign of life, and it was clear that he was in excruciating pain. Although it was easy for me to detach myself from his predicament, I felt a cold chill run through my body when he looked directly at me from his swollen, bloody eyes and begged me to vouch for his innocence. Terry began to sob loudly, and most of the crew members turned their heads away from the grotesque sight. A tough-looking young man who looked to be no more than thirty years old came forward and grabbed me by the arm. He pulled me close to where Jacan was hanging and placed a pistol in my hand. He told me that as an apology to me from the organization, I was being given the honor of killing the man who tried to get me killed. By this time, Jacan's body had gone limp, but from the slight movement of his chest as he struggled to breathe, it was clear that he was still alive.

I declined the honor of becoming a murderer, even though a quick death would've been an act of mercy. After a long pause, Darren stepped forward, took the gun out of my hand, and shot

Jacan three times in the chest. I could see that he didn't take pleasure in the act. My senses told me that not only did he want to end Jacan's suffering, he also wanted to get me off the hook of having to do it. I expected that there would be some kind of movie-style speech afterward, something like, 'This is what you get when you fuck with the organization.' But there was nothing. Everyone just dispersed and went on their way.

Maybe that speech was already made before I got there, or maybe with me being the grieved party, they didn't believe I needed to be there for it.

After everyone but the clean-up crew had left, Darren and I stood there awhile. It was only then that I saw the bodies littering the floor in the corner of the room. They found the entire crew and eliminated them all. Darren was still slightly shaken, but he maintained a good front. I turned to him, shook his hand, and thanked him. He appreciated my understanding of what he had done for both me and Jacan. When we got back to the car, Darren told me what had transpired in the warehouse before I arrived and what had been happening for the last week.

Jacan had been continually telling anyone who would listen that he thought I had set up the robbery. His biggest mistake was saying that I was the one who decided to circumvent the usual procedure for the drop and take him along. Fortunately, I had the presence of mind to call Mr. Walker before going along with his misguided caper. I was on record with the deviation, so the organization focused in on Jacan like a laser to expose the gang that ripped them off. His brother lobbied to spare his life, but as more and more details came out, it was clear that Jacan was an ongoing danger to the organization and his brother. Jacan had run up a large debt with a couple of local gangs; the money was spent on his growing cocaine habit. One of the gang leaders approached him with the robbery scheme, but Jacan refused. He knew that they wouldn't do anything too drastic to him, knowing who his brother was. But in desperation, Jacan tried to rob a local jeweler and was immediately caught. He pretended to have a gun in his pocket when he approached the jeweler at the counter. Jacan was lucky that the armed off-duty cop, who was a customer at the time, didn't kill him. The entire station got a good laugh out of it, but when one of the detectives realized who Jacan was, more importantly, who his brother was, they made him believe that he was facing a long prison sentence and got him to cooperate. Jacan was too stupid or too coked up to know that any low-level public defender could've easily squashed an attempted robbery with a finger charge by a person with no priors. It definitely could've been easily handled by the talented defense attorneys the organization had under their employ. Maybe Jacan felt that he had way too many fuck ups to bring this one back to his brother. On one occasion, the cops wired him up for a meeting with his brother, but he never made it to the meeting. He decided to cop some coke first to put his nerves at ease, but the dealer that supplied him noticed the wire and thought he was setting them up. To save his own life, Jacan convinced them that he was working with the cops, but against the organization, not them. They believed him and saw this as a great opportunity to blackmail him into setting up the robbery that they had failed to get him to do earlier. When all of this came to light, the organization started setting the stage to eliminate the gang with Jacan and set them up as the perpetrators. They convinced Jacan to get the gang members back at the warehouse by telling them the organization was storing a shit load of drugs and money there. It's ironic how the most cunning of thieves turn into idiots when greed kicks in. Jacan got the bulk of the guys who participated in the robbery to come and gave the organization the names and locations of the two who wouldn't be there. Those two were picked up shortly after the others left for the warehouse. Jacan and the three top gang members (the ones who never left their car during the robbery) were separated from the rest of the group, who were immediately killed in a barrage of gunfire. The three leaders and Jacan were tied down and mercilessly beaten with a bat by the guy who offered me the kill. The crew members were forced to spike-nail them to the wall while they screamed in agony. It must've been a soul-wrenching thing for them to do. These guys were drug dealers and petty thieves, not sadistic torturers. Darren then hit me with some news that shook me to the core, which wasn't easy after all that I had just heard. The guy who threw the vicious beating on the top three gang members and Jacan was Jacan's brother. Amon was held responsible for his brother's actions and had to make a gritty gesture to prove his resolve to protect the organization. when I refused the "honor" of the kill, he was the one who had to do it. So, Darren's gesture wasn't all altruistic after all; by finishing off Jacan, he also ingratiated himself with his brother Amon. Either way, Darren did all three of us a favor by taking on that gruesome responsibility.

CHAPTER SIX

The Calm Before The Storm

Things had cooled down a bit, and the cops bought the idea that Jacan, being the fuck up that he was, went to buy drugs with their wire on and initiated a wild gun battle between two gang factions. The organization executed a half dozen rival gang members and staged the warehouse to push that narrative, and the cops accepted it. Terry disappeared from the scene. It was no surprise to me, after seeing her visceral response to that gruesome scene at the warehouse, that she would re-evaluate her entire life. It deeply affected me, and I'm a borderline sociopath.

Darren and I were given higher positions in the organization. Darren was given the spot of negotiator and problem solver; in laymen's language, he became the deal-maker and enforcer. He laid out the organization's terms with new clients and enforced their compliance. I had no idea what space I was filling or what it was called. I acted as an executive secretary of sorts to My Walker and shadowed him on some of his excursions. I was given a small but posh office in the Highrise where the organization had an entire floor. Between assisting Mr. Walker, I spent hours in the office combing over some of the organization's holdings and positions in legitimate companies. I wasn't checking numbers or receipts; my job was to search for hidden opportunities. I Finally realized what position I was in while riding up in the elevator with one of the organization's managerial staff, he addressed me as Mr. Gould. It was clear to me that I was now the young protégé of Mr. Walker. It didn't take long before I found out how wide-ranging his duties were. I sat in on one meeting with him, an act that was formally protested by several of the attendees, but after Mr. Walker overruled them, they yielded without another word or a single side-eye.

The meeting was to decide whether or not to take out a client who had repeatedly broken protocol and exposed the organization to the scrutiny of the Feds. I was beginning to believe that the other committee members were right; I shouldn't have been there. Even as a pretender to Mr. Walker's throne, if I was supposed to be there, why not Darren? He was responsible for everything that would've led up to this meeting and possibly the action that would come next after that display he made in the warehouse with Jacan. It was decided that the client would be "removed' and Mr. Walker was the member who personally took care of all the high-profile hits. I have to admit that I didn't see this coming. Mr. Walker was the Consigliere, Manager, and what they called "an Adjuster". More disturbingly, I knew he would drag me along. He knew that I wasn't a killer, but after my actions at the warehouse, he also knew that I wasn't squeamish about those sorts of things.

CHAPTER SEVEN

Archies Fatal Mistake

The client was an independent dealer and businessman, he operated out of his butcher shop by wrapping the packages in large cuts of various animal parts. Archie ran a tight and seamless operation, making nearly as much selling meat as he did selling the product that was stuffed in the meat. The payment was negotiated and paid for at different locations, and the product was picked up at the shop. Archie even charged the people he sold the product to for the meat it was wrapped in. He always told them that it looked better if people saw them paying like everyone else, but he gave up that farce the day he argued with a client who was a few dollars short of the cost of the meat. The client was livid that instead of a quick in and out, he had customers staring as Archie berated him for coming up short on a sixty-five-dollar meat purchase with six thousand dollars of cocaine inside. Archie was reckless on several occasions. One day, a regular customer ordered a quarter slab of Pig for a barbeque, and Archie mistakenly gave him one of the hot packages, as he called them. The customer was already in his car and about to take off before Archie chased him down and blubbered out some nonsensical excuse about mixing up orders. The customer was irate about going through the trouble of unpacking a large slab of pig from his car just to exchange it for the exact same thing. He kept asking Archie why he couldn't just give the other customer the one he ordered. When Archie got the hot package back in the store, he realized he didn't have another quarter slab, so he had to remove the package and give the customer back the same piece of meat. The customer noticed it was the same, and after another blubbering excuse of the other guy canceling and he wasn't informed, the customer vowed never to return. All that time, other customers waited in line to be served, listening to the entire ridiculous exchange.

Archie's Fatal mistake was using the organization's reputation to strong-arm his customers into paying unreasonable price hikes. When they complained, he told them that the organization was constantly raising prices and threatening him to pay, so he had to pass on the cost. When distributors and dealers started griping with each other, this put too much chatter in the streets. Mr. Walker intercepted a disgruntled customer of Archie just before he could drop a dime in retaliation. One of his contacts got news of this impending disaster and brought it to him. It took a lot of damage control to set everyone straight about Archie's lies. Darren and his crew were working overtime to get things back in order, I found out that was the reason he wasn't at that last meeting. Archie's greed had made him a serious liability and a marked man.

Mr. Walker had already made one trip to the shop and found it closed in the middle of the day. Archie had found out about his impending demise and cleared out with anything he could carry. He must've been prepared for this inevitability because his bank account was cleared out, and the apartment above the store where he lived had all the utility accounts closed. You would think this entire situation would've taught Archie something, but you'd be wrong. Mr. Walker knew exactly how to expose Archie without chasing him across the country. He told me that a good hunter never chases his prey; he gets his prey to come to him. I hesitantly asked him how he planned to get a marked man to come to his own end voluntarily. He dawned a wry grin and said, "You don't crawl into the hole to catch a rat; you put out a piece of cheese." It was an easy enough concept for anyone to grasp, but I just didn't see any chance of Archie exposing himself after going on the run. I don't believe I've ever seen Mr. Walker's face show any sign of any pleasant emotions, and that disturbing grin he exhibited didn't qualify as a positive change in his facial pattern.

CHAPTER EIGHT

Baiting The Trap

While working closely with Mr. Walker, he informed me about his plan to lure Archie out of hiding; although I found it incredulous, who was I to second guess someone who had mastered his craft over decades of implementation? It was just so rudimentary that I couldn't bring myself to believe that anyone would be dimwitted enough to fall for it, but I soon realized the immense power that greed had over logic and self-preservation for some people. Through contacts, we learned where the closest thing to family Archie had lived in the city and then laid out the cheese for the rat to bite.

John and Archie grew up in the same neighborhood and were virtually inseparable most of their young lives. They had a similar appearance, so everyone always thought they were brothers. Archie's mother liked John, and at times, his Father treated John better than he did Archie. When Archie's father was in the hospital dying of lung disease, he had the two of them come to the hospital, where he confessed to them that they were indeed half-brothers. Archie was less shocked by the news than John was, and neither of the mothers expressed any surprise. It was clear that they both knew for a long time. Archie and John's bond became stronger than ever. They started realizing that they were more alike than they had ever noticed before. They took over their father's butcher shop and gave both mothers the carefree life that they deserved.

The shop kept them financially sound while their mothers were alive; after both mothers had passed on, they were making enough money to afford a life of modest luxury but nowhere near enough to satisfy either of these money-grubbing half-brothers. They just couldn't see themselves working as hard as they did without seeing bigger returns. The economy started to falter, and inflation started to affect their bottom line. They didn't buy the building that the shop was in when the money was available because the rent was low based on the economy of the neighborhood, but like many places in the city, gentrification was setting in, and the influx of young professionals enticed the owner to nearly double the rent. When Archie was approached by a local crew with the proposition of selling product out of their shop, he was hesitant. Archie didn't see it as a moral or ethical dilemma, it was all about logistics and risk vs reward. When the dealer laid out the entire plan with the amount of money guaranteed on Archie and John's end, Archie quickly pounced on it. John was impressed by the deal, but he had already spent a small stretch in prison years ago for seriously injuring a couple of people while driving under the influence, and he vowed never again to do anything that would jeopardize his freedom. The dealer gave Archie a big advance, and he used most of it to buy out John.

Mr. Walker also got the complete list of Archie's clients and found out that one of them was sitting on twenty grand that he never got a chance to get to Archie. He was the same guy who first approached Archie and got him into the business, as well as the one who introduced Archie to the organization. It took little persuasion to get the dealer to go along with the Organization's plan to get to Archie. By bringing Archie into the fold, the dealer felt he might also be held accountable for Archie's transgressions. Mr. Walker got the dealer to approach John with the twenty grand while pretending not to know about his flight for life. He just dropped the money off with John and told him that he couldn't locate Archie and didn't want to jeopardize future shipments because of one missed payment. The dealer never asked John a single question; he just dropped the money and left. John didn't hesitate to take the money. He knew that it was more than likely a ploy to pull Archie out of hiding, but greed told him that he was smart enough to either get it to Archie safely, minus his cut, or just keep it all and never tell Archie.

John wrestled with what action to take for a week; all that time, Darren had one of his crew members watching him like a hawk, day and night. I wondered aloud if it was worth all the time and money the organization was expending to make an example out of one worn-out old butcher. Mr. Walker told me that the numbers had been computed long before either of us was born. "Letting this go unanswered would be more costly than ten times the amount of money and manpower that the organization had spent up to this point." I began to understand the logic of gang warfare.

One day, Archie contacted John out of the blue, asking him if anyone had approached him to inquire about his location. Archie had just remembered that John was present when he made that first deal in the shop and was worried that John might be in danger. When John told him about the twenty grand, Archie lit up, forgetting about all of his troubles. He had more than enough money on hand to get away and start a new life but couldn't resist the idea of having more. Archie even haggled with John about how much his cut should be. They spent a half hour discussing the split and another hour figuring out how to safely get the money to Archie. He never asked about the demeanor of the dealer who delivered the money or if John had noticed any strange people or vehicles hanging around his house. This wasn't new for Archie or John; they had tunnel vision when it came to money.

The plan was for John to spend the day driving around town, stopping at several stores to check for anyone tailing him, then he would walk to the butcher shop using the back alleys and entering from the rear. Archie was sure this plan would work to expose anyone following John. The plan had a major flaw. No one was ever following John. Darren had a crew member staked out in a house with a clear view of John's house and one in an apartment in the building right next to the shop, from which there was an unobstructed view of the front and back entrances. Mr. Walker knew that Archie would use one of those two places where he had a false sense of security.

When Darren received word that John had left the house from his man who was staking it out and news from workers in a couple of stores owned by the organization that John was spotted shopping, buying randomly odd items. Darren had decided to spend that night staking out the store personally. He reported it to Mr. Walker, and he agreed that it would probably be happening tonight and at that location. John was doing his best I spy impersonation as he snaked through the back alleys, and his fumbling with keys to open the back door of the shop while frantically looking around into the darkness was so comical that it made Darren laugh loud enough to be heard through the closed double pane window. Mr. Walker sat quietly in a chair near Darren, cleaning his nails with a small file, and I nervously paced the room in anticipation of what was to come.

CHAPTER NINE

The Butcher Butchered

Darren kept staring at Mr. Walker, wondering when we were going to spring the trap, but Mr. Walker continued with his nail grooming as if he was about to start a hand modeling session. Darren turned his gaze on me, I just shrugged my shoulders. I was just as clueless as he was. There was a light tapping on the door, and Mr. Walker suddenly rose out of his chair and said, "It's time".

It was Amon at the door. A cold chill ran down my spine. I knew this was going to become gruesome and that it would be very messy because of the nature of the betrayal and the amount of reputational damage it caused. Seeing Amon brought back memories of the horrid scene at the warehouse where his brother was killed. We all slowly walked down the stairs like a funeral procession, never saying a word or making a sound. We entered the back of the shop just as John had done and found him sitting on a chair unbound, crying profusely and begging for his life. John had one small cut on the side of his forehead, which had a thin line of blood running down from it. His sobbing was loud at intervals but muted most of the time. Amon warned him to keep it down, promising another crack across his skull. I was mentally ready to see Archie get his due, but as far as I knew, John was just a greedy idiot who got caught up in Archie's mess. I couldn't see a way for him to get out of this alive, and that really troubled me. Mr. Walker and Amon quietly conversed about the situation. John was grabbed the minute he entered the shop and had gone through a vicious interrogation. I didn't understand why John had to die, which was clearly the direction things were going. After expressing my concerns with Mr. Walker, it all became clear.

He told me that John had brought himself into the situation by taking the money and contacting Archie. No one wanted John dead, but he was a serious loose end that couldn't be ignored. Archie was brought into the store from the back; he was picked up earlier while en route to the store and brought to a different location to be questioned. I was surprised that he didn't have a scratch on him. It was also surprising that Archie didn't seem concerned at all about his predicament, he was either accepting his fate with grace and courage, or he found a way to satisfy the organization and save both his and John's life. Neither seemed plausible to me. Any hopes that I had were quickly dashed when Amon gave Archie a vicious hit across his skull with the butt of his pistol, giving him a nearly identical wound as John. Archie collapsed to the floor but was immediately yanked up like a rag doll by one of Darren's men. Mr. Walker Placed an armless wooden chair next to John and motioned the crew member to sit Archie in it. Both of them sat unbound with blood on their faces. John continued to plead for his life, but Archie stayed silent. His face started to show the concern warranted by the situation. Everyone else was silent; whatever information the organization needed from Archie was already obtained at the prior location where he was questioned.

The only decision left at this point was how to dispatch Archie, sending the strongest message to anyone who had any thoughts of betraying the organization and what to do with John.

Everyone started moving away from Archie towards one side of the room, Darren dragged John while still in his chair as he joined the others. Amon moved forward towards Archie, and the brutal beating started so fast I doubt if anyone saw the first few blows. Amon had given his gun to one of the crew members and began plummeting Archie with his fists. Archie was quickly knocked to the floor where Amon switched from Mike Tyson mode to Bruce Lee and began kicking Archie mercilessly. After that, he went into WWF mode and began tossing Archie around like a rag doll, ending with a long agonizing choke hold. John cried and begged until he didn't have enough breath to continue. From the faces of the others, I knew that the horror wasn't over yet; there was still John to deal with. I didn't know that during the time before we entered the shop, John had been given an offer that would've saved his life but refused. As Amon began to walk toward him, John began to frantically scream, "I'll do it! I'll do it!" He was drenched in sweat, and snot covered the lower part of his face.

We all went into an adjacent room around a large wooden table, and Amon dropped Archie's lifeless body on top of it spread eagle. Darren handed John a pair of heavy rubber gloves and a long black neoprene apron from a nearby shelf. John sobbed and whimpered as he donned the items. It became clear that the deal made with John was for him to dismember the body for disposal, making him an accessory after the fact. This supposedly gave the organization cover from John going to the cops, But I couldn't see the logic behind it. He could always say he was threatened with death, and I don't think there is a specific law against cutting up a dead body. I don't think John realized how lucky he was, this was an unprecedented gift from the organization. It was an act of leniency that I never expected, but the organization's plan was much more devious than I had imagined. As John started the first cut at the elbow joint of Archie's left arm, Archie jerked back into consciousness with a bellowing scream. John jumped back in horror with the bone saw still in his hand, and the steady buzzing from it accompanied Archie's screams, forming a symphony of terror. Amon quickly pressed the gun to John's temple and yelled at him to continue. Hesitantly, John moved forward with his eyes half-opened and filled with tears; he mangled Archie's limbs with misplaced cuts until the screaming stopped, and the only sound left was the humming of the blade.

Amon handed John a large cleaver off of a nearby rack and told him, "Get this over with; we don't have all night." Although John's face was still covered with a mixture of sweat, tears, mucus, and Archie's blood, he mustered the strength or resignation to compose himself. He methodically dismembered Archie's body with all the skill and expertise of his trade. I have to admit that the whole scene went from disgusting to educational. Everyone seemed engrossed in the well-ordered procedure John took to complete his task. Darren's crew was responsible for packing the pieces and cleaning up the residual mess. John sat quietly in a state of shock, still in his bloody attire, until Darren awakened him from his stupor to clean and sterilize it and him. Although John saved his life by participating in this gruesome cleansing of old business, he was not free from the clutches of the organization. He was forced into reopening the shop and continuing with the distribution of product, but Mr. Walker made sure to keep him under strict supervision to avoid another Archie-styled disaster. I had no doubt that after this morbid scene, John would be called on in the future for more than just product distribution.

CHAPTER TEN

Disturbing Developments

Things were quiet for months, and business was doing well when another potentially disastrous situation reared its ugly head. Amon, who had been a stable force of strength for the organization, had become excessively violent and erratic. A few of his crew members had approached Mr. Walker at different times, expressing their concern about Amon's behavioral decline, but their concerns were quickly dismissed as anomalies. When Amon took it upon himself to take out a crew member of a business associate without any discussion or permission from the organization, it was clear that the problem was far greater than Mr. Walker had imagined. The killing had taken place in the organization's best and most secure location, the warehouse, which was already under intense scrutiny by law enforcement after the last horrific incident. Mr. Walker had insulated the organization from the warehouse with a series of business transfers and creative paperwork, but now it was rendered useless. Surveillance by cops during the impending investigation made it too hot to ever do business in it again, and finding a location that served them as well and as long as the warehouse wouldn't be easy. The situation became more dire when Amon went dark. He hadn't been seen or heard from since the incident. If he came in and made a case for why such a drastic measure had to be taken, it could've all been worked out in some manner, but just disappearing from the scene implied that he knew there was no excuse for what he had done, and that he feared the consequences of his action. This made him a threat of exposing the organization to the authorities. There was even talk of him possibly cooperating with the cops to get out of his predicament, but no one believed Amon would go that far; then again, they never believed that he would've ever put himself in the position he was at this moment. Just the fact that a highly stationed member was A.W.O.L. and a possible threat created a problem. Not only for the organization, but also for everyone who had dealt directly with him in the past. Mr. Walker had to call in vouchers and make a multitude of threats to keep nervous clients at bay long enough to give Amon a bit of time to come to his senses. They reluctantly agreed to Mr. Walker's strong "requests" but made it clear that their patience was short, and time was already running out.

It became clear that the decline in Amon's behavior started shortly after he was forced into bludgeoning his own brother in that warehouse nearly a year ago. He became short-tempered with his crew members, physically assaulting one for questioning an unusual order and threatening one with his gun for a perceived lack of respect after a pointed joke. These were common practices among many of the gangs the organization dealt with, but it was not something they tolerated within their operation. Mr. Walker would've quickly acted to neutralize anyone who had put themselves in the position Amon was now, without regard to their past performance or level of engagement with the organization, but he blamed himself for not taking the complaints that were brought to him earlier by Amon's crew members seriously. He believed that if he had properly assessed the situation then, all of this could've been averted. Mr. Walker had long heard about the unsanctioned meeting but didn't think it was serious enough to stop it from happening. He believed he owed it to Amon to try and get this all cleared up without him losing his life. He also had some reservations about the validity of it all. He never vocalized it to anyone, but he had noticed a bit of comradery between Amon and Dilion and couldn't see how their relationship could've declined this quickly and to fatal ends. Of course, that didn't mean much in this business; Mr. Walker had seen many people killed by supposed friends in his long career.

News of the disruption in the organization quickly spread to the streets, and the word was that the cops were mounting their own search for Amon. They were initially after him just for the murder, but after an intensive investigation, they learned more about the situation than the organization had been able to uncover.

Dilion was a top negotiator for a crew that the organization had been doing business with for nearly a decade but cut ties with them when they started taking contract hits as a part of their operation. Their separation from the organization cut them out of many lucrative drug deals. Although the organization didn't forbid other crews to keep doing business with them, their added venture brought too many risks to continue directly associating with them. When Dilion cut ties with that crew and started his own operation, the organization agreed to keep him in the fold as long as he didn't do any direct business with his old gang. He agreed and was allowed out of the gang for ten percent of his take. Other than passing them that envelope every month, he had no obligation to have any other contact with them. Both the organization and Dilion's old crew found those terms acceptable.

This worked out well for everyone until Dilion was approached by another crew because of his past contacts with people willing to make high-risk hits for reasonable sums of money. Dilion refused at first, but with a combination of the large sum he was offered for just making the introduction and the promise of the exclusive rights to future coke deals within their operation, Dilion agreed to the deal under the exception that they would never approach him about any contract hits in the future, and that this would never get back to the organization or his old crew.

If it got back to the organization, he would be cut out of the loop just like his old crew was. If it got back to his old crew, they would not only consider it a breach of their agreement, but he would also be betraying them by helping another crew cut into what was now a large part of their operation. The deal went through without a hitch, and Dilion continued his regular operation. It all began to fall apart when the hitter the crew hired was killed during a different assignment, and they needed a replacement. they broke the agreement and asked Dilion for another introduction. This time no amount of money would sway him, and he didn't care if he lost their business in the drug trade. He knew that the first deal was a mistake but took the calculated risk that one introduction was worth the risk for the added business, but at this point, going any further would be a stupid move. That's when the crew resorted to blackmail, threatening to destroy his whole operation by outing the introduction. They also promised to add a few plausible lies to the mix. Dilion was incensed. The gang gave him a few days to make a decision.

CHAPTER ELEVEN

Amon's Dilemma

Dilion became desperate. He knew that going any further down the rabbit hole would end in disaster. He had built up a close working relationship with Amon when he was with the old gang, which continued after he separated from them and formed his new crew. Their relationship was the closest either of them had to a legitimate friendship. Dilion sent a message to Amon requesting an unsanctioned meeting. Amon, under normal circumstances would've never agreed to a meeting with any client or associate without prior approval from the organization. He arranged a call to speak directly to Dilion to reject his request, but after hearing the concern in Dilion's voice, Amon knew that the subject would be of a serious nature, and any serious concern that Dilion had would definitely affect the organization. He chose to grant the meeting based on that; at least that's what he told Dilion. But truth be told, after his brother's death Amon felt lost. He didn't feel remorse or regret about his part in the murder, it was something that had to be done under the circumstances. Amon's anguish was heightened because he felt that if he hadn't constantly protected his brother every time he screwed up and if he allowed him to face the consequences of his actions, it would've never gone as far as it did. The entire reason he brought Jacan into the organization was to keep him out of trouble, but putting him in constant close proximity to readily available drugs is what got him hooked and eventually killed. The real reason Amon agreed to the unsanctioned meeting was because Dilion was the only person left with whom he felt any personal bond; it was like a second chance to help a little brother out of a serious jam. He had been very rough on his crew lately and thought he could get some closure by helping Dilion out of whatever mess he was in.

They met at the same warehouse where most of the organization's business was done. Mr. Walker had really done his homework in finding and procuring this location. Over a decade in operation, and it has never been compromised. It was secured in every respect. They had a small hidden location with signal jammers that worked on cameras and electronic communications. The paperwork was clean, and the location was isolated from prying eyes.

Amon got there first and paced through the large open area just inside the wide steel doors, he was remembering the tragic day he lost Jacan. Dilion arrived a half hour later. Amon and Dilion shook hands with uncharacteristic smiles on both of their faces. They moved to one corner of the room and sat on a narrow ledge protruding from the wall. Before getting to the business at hand, Dilion reminisced about their first meeting at the warehouse. He was just getting his start with the crew, and they let him lead the negotiation. He thought it was some kind of hazing ritual, but as he spoke with Amon, he realized how serious it all was. Amon was stoic as they hammered out the terms of a deal that were spoon-fed to Dilion for over a week to make him look credible. Dilion was placed out front in case the deal went sour. They would use him as the fall guy.

But he parroted his lines out perfectly and even improvised with a fix to a concerning snag in the deal not anticipated by his gang leader. Although Dilion kept his composure at the time, Amon could see his nervousness and did everything he could to help him stay focused. Amon looked at it as helping the deal get done, but he saw himself in this young upstart and was already feeling more than just a professional connection. Dilion was the kind of person he had wanted Jacan to be.

After that short trip down memory lane, Dilion told Amon the entire story. Amon was less concerned about it than Dilion thought he would be. Amon explained that it wouldn't be hard to square such a small transgression with the organization. It would just involve a small sanction and a bit of structured oversight. After all, he didn't hide any of the profits from that new alliance, and they wouldn't consider one introduction a reason to cut ties with someone who was bringing the kind of money Dilion was bringing in for the organization. But keeping it from being an issue with his old gang was a bit trickier. Over eighty percent of their business was now from extortion, which relied heavily on their ability to collect with strong-arming and hits. Dilion essentially moved one of their highest earners to a major competitor. He also didn't know that the hitter was working for his old gang at that time, and the introduction was a ruse to expose him for elimination. Dilion had literally handed him over to the rival crew.

Amon told Dilion that he would have to bring it to the organization and see if there was any way they could help, but Amon and Dilion were going to have to come up with some very convincing scenarios of why it would undoubtedly be in their best interest to do so.

The warehouse doors suddenly opened, and they were face to face with three pistol-wielding guys; Dilion immediately recognized them as members of the crew who had approached him with the ultimatum. Dilion was extremely careful about avoiding tails but didn't realize that they had installed a tracker on his car. Amon and Dilion were pushed back into the warehouse, and the doors were closed and locked. After the gang's leader, (Balde) searched them and took their weapons, he spent nearly an hour trying to convince Amon and Dilion to quietly go along with their plan using threats of exposure and death, but they both knew that death would be the eventual result of any decision they made. Amon noticed that the youngest-looking member of the crew was easily distracted; he spent a good amount of time scanning the warehouse with a curious gaze. He was also the closest to Amon, and the gun in his hand was always lazily held, with his arm dangling at the side of his body closest to Amon. Amon continued to look for an opportunity to turn the tables as Balde vainly pitched his proposal. Dilion was aware of what Amon was thinking, but his only chance at successfully taking any action was in support of any move Amon made. Balde had stopped talking, knowing that he wasn't getting anywhere. Amon noticed that the other two guys were looking away, so he took the opportunity to yank the weapon out of the hands of the young crew member. His grip was so light on the weapon that it dropped to the floor before Amon quickly scooped it up and dispatched him and the other distracted crew member. Dilion and Balde were wrestling for control of his weapon.

When Amon attempted to shoot Balde to help Dilion, the gun misfired; as he quickly moved in to physically help Dilion, a shot rang out. Amon looked directly into Dilion's sad, dying eyes as his body slowly crumpled to the cold, hard floor. Amon froze for a moment before realizing the danger he was still in. Fortunately, Blade was clutching his ringing ears because of how close they were to the weapon when it went off. Amon quickly snapped himself back into reality and dashed for cover as bullets whizzed by. He could hear the clicking from the empty gun as he moved behind some heavy wooden crates in one corner of the room, but he knew that there were still three loaded guns somewhere out there. Amon peeked around the crates just in time to catch a round in his right shoulder. He quickly ducked back behind the stacked crates. Balde slowly approached the crates to finish the job, but Amon mustered all the strength that he had left to tip the crates over on top of Balde. He knew he was in no condition to fight further, so he made a mad dash for the warehouse door. He could hear Balde's bellowing screams as he attempted to free himself from under the heavy crates.

Amon made it out of the warehouse and shuffled his way through a wooded section following alongside the roadside. He knew that he couldn't risk being picked up by just anyone. Although his wound wasn't life-threatening, Amon had lost more blood than he had realized and was getting weaker. He knew that blacking out in the woods was not a viable option, so he decided to take a chance flagging down someone on the road. After making it to the side of the road, Amon walked alongside it, hoping to get lucky with a driver who wouldn't ask too many questions. He had enough money to bribe someone to take him where he wanted to go, but there was no guarantee of who he would end up with. Things slowly went black, and Amon collapsed on the side of the road.

Inside the warehouse, Balde had freed himself from under the crates. He quickly called in a clean-up squad to clear away all signs of his crew ever being there. Balde knew that Amon couldn't get too far with his injuries; that would give him enough time to get rid of the bodies of his men and set the stage with his contingency plan. If Amon and Dilion didn't go along with his scheme. The plan was to kill Dilion with Amon's gun, take over his territory, and blackmail Amon with the killing. Everyone knew about Amon's recent violent and erratic behavior, and Balde had secured a couple of associates to swear that they heard Amon threaten to kill Dilion. He cleaned Amon's weapon of prints and tossed it in some bushes very close to the warehouse where even the most inept of cops could find it. Earlier, when Balde had relieved them of their weapons, he holstered his own and held onto theirs. After killing Dilion with Amon's gun and running out of bullets trying to kill Amon, in a moment of clarity, Balde used Dilion's gun to wound Amon. So they both had bullets from each other's guns inside them. Balde wiped Dilion's weapon clean and placed it back into his lifeless hands. Even with the original scenario going to shit, the plan was still solidly holding up.

The hunt for Amon was at a feverish pace. Cops scoured the city searching for him. The organization had multiple crews on alert, and some of their associates had informed them that they could no longer sit on their hands in the matter. Mr. Walker no longer had any control over Amon's fate.

CHAPTER TWELVE

An Angel of Mercy

Dara Had finally escaped the dull monotony of farm life. She had long promised herself that when she came of age, she would jump into that old clinker that her uncle had pieced together for her and ride into the wind. She had her life savings of three hundred dollars in her pocket and a promise from that same uncle to get more to her as soon as she found a place to settle into. Her parents were kind and gentle, religious people of good temperament who spent their lives working their farm and attending church on a regular basis. Dara knew that she was never meant to be a slave to religion or spend her life working in the fields. With no clear destination in mind, Dara barreled down the road without a care in the world. She was just five feet- five inches, not fat, but she had a solid, strong body from years of hard labor. Her fiery red hair and bright freckles made her stand out in a crowd, but no more than her bright, cheery disposition. Dara was fearless and longed for much more than farm life could give her. Her uncle had traveled the world as a soldier and wanted to help Dara spread her wings and experience as much of the world as possible. With the radio blaring her favorite song, competing with the roar of the wind that blew through the windows she refused to shut, Dara headed straight into those possibilities.

Suddenly, Dara screeched on the brakes, barely stopping her old hooptie. She checked her mirror for any other traffic on the empty road and slowly backed up. There was a body just off the side of the road. Dara jumped out to check and see if the person was alive. As she gently touched the shoulder of the prone, downward-faced body, it jerked in pain. Dara gently rolled the person over to see that his shirt was bloody around the right shoulder area; as she loosened his shirt, she could see the small bullet hole. This was not a sight foreign to Dara. Her Uncle had regaled her with stories of combat and combat wounds for the last five years. He even let her tag along to the local mortuary to visit his old Army buddy Mort, who had made it his trade after retiring from the military. As long as she promised not to tell her parents, they both allowed her to witness some of the autopsies Mort performed. Mort even gave Dara an authentic medical triage kit that she used diligently on her dolls and, occasionally, on dead rodents found in the fields of their farm. Dara was a trooper from the start. She had a strong constitution and never experienced any ill effects from dealing with death.

Dara checked for an exit wound but didn't find one. The bullet was still inside and not very deep. Amon flailed for a moment, not knowing what was happening, but Dara put him at ease by telling him she was a nurse. Another trick she learned from her uncle. He told her that a panicked person could be put at ease just by telling them that you're an expert on whatever they were panicking about. It makes them feel that they are in safe hands.

Amon Immediately asked her to take him to one of the organization's safe houses. He told her that he had money in his pocket to pay her and much more later if she helped him. Dara told him that he needed to get to a hospital right away because he had lost a lot of blood, and the bullet and material from his shirt had to be removed from the wound before it became infected. Amon repeated his pleas before blacking out.

Dara had no idea how to get to the address Amon had given her, and she knew that a hospital would have just as many questions for her as they would for him. She struggled to get the unconscious Amon into her car and drove on, undecided about what to do until she saw a secluded motel on the side of the road. She went in and got a room. Luckily there was no activity outside to notice Amon passed out in her car. She got a room far away from the office entrance and literally dragged Amon into it. All Dara could think of was what would happen if he died and who would believe her story. After getting Amon into the room and onto one of the twin beds, Dara rushed back to the car for her triage kit.

Amon regained consciousness as the morning sun rose and brightened the motel room. After a long night of needed rest, he awakened to find his wound cleaned and dressed. He got his first clear look at Dara and thanked her profusely for helping him and not exposing him to the scrutiny of the authorities by taking him to a hospital. Dara told Amon that she had removed the bullet and then handed it to him.

Dara sterilized and stitched up the wound. She told Amon that although he wouldn't need any further care, he would be weak from all the blood he had lost, and it would be better if he had a course of antibiotics.

Amon immediately called Mr. Walker and explained the entire situation to him. Mr. Walker told him to stay put until he could get a firm handle on everyone who was on the hunt for him. Mr. Walker immediately informed the organization about everything Amon told him.

After getting all of the organization's clients and associates to stand down, the next order of business was to figure out a way to get Amon off the hook with the cops. They also had to deal with Balde in a manner that would deter anyone from ever trying something like this again. Balde's crew was disbanded and integrated into other gangs; none of them faced any repercussions because they acted under the orders from Balde, who was now on the run and in hiding.

Two of the organization's top lawyers immediately got busy with a defense for Amon. They were very optimistic after getting all of the information the police had from their investigation. Amon was quickly listed as an employee of one of the shadow companies attached to the warehouse. They planned to portray Amon as a victim in a blotched robbery perpetrated by Balde and Dilion. The gun that the cops found near the warehouse would match the bullet taken from Dilion's body, but it couldn't be traced back to Amon. The only body on the scene was Dilion's because Balde had his crew member's bodies removed, and Balde's DNA was found all over it from their struggle for the weapon. Although police knew Amon was a well-established member of a criminal organization, he only had two sealed nonviolent arrests as a juvenile. Balde, on the other hand, had an extensive arrest record with multiple assaults and one attempted murder charge that he had pled down. Mr. Walker was also able to locate the couple Balde had paid to come forward as witnesses if needed. They gave sworn depositions of the proposed plan set up by Balde, leaving out any information they had about Amon. The lawyers informed the cops about Amon's struggle to reach help before blacking out in the woods and the kind stranger who picked him up and chose to address his wounds because she didn't know the area and was afraid that he was too near death for her to drive around blindly looking for a hospital.

Two patrol cars rolled into the motel parking area with their lights on but no sirens. Mr. Walker and one of the organization's lawyers were there before them to brief Amon and Dara. The cops wanted to handcuff Aman and take him in for questioning at the station, but the lawyer cautioned them of serious litigation if they injured him further by bouncing him down the rough road in a patrol car. They decided to call for an ambulance and transport him directly to the hospital. The cops handcuffed Amon to the gurney despite his weakened state, he was still a suspect in a murder, regardless of all the contrary information the cops had gathered.

The case against Amon quickly disintegrated to the point that Prosecutors refused to bring charges. The D.A. told the cops that they would be laughed out of court with the case they had tried to build against Amon. The hunt for Balde continued by all sides, but he was never found. Word on the street was that a few of the organization's associates wanted the matter to disappear but knew that the organization would complicate matters by making a public display of Balde's death just to send a message, so they found him and dispatched him quietly.

Associates and members at all levels in the organization were happy that Amon was fully exonerated and back in good standing. He was a great asset to them all, but for now, Amon had to lay low until the heat from local authorities waned. It wouldn't be long before he could be back in action; cops quickly redirected their focus to other cases of gang violence, which was on the rise. When it came to the murder of known gang members, their only interest was getting citations for arrests and convictions. Getting justice for the victims was never an priority because they weren't considered victims, just casualties of their own trade.

CHAPTER THIRTEEN

Looking Hard For A Way Out

All of the turmoil was taking a toll on me, I started having anxiety attacks almost daily. I'd been filling in for Amon during the entire ordeal and had my own share of close catastrophes. While directing Amon's crew I made a series of decisions that had them all ready to revolt. They were used to Amon's style of leadership and took offense at having to take directions from a young novice who had not long ago entered their domain. At one point, Mr. Walker had to intervene to get them back in line; at that time, he expressed his disappointment with me for not being able to keep them straight with all the authority I was given. The first sign of discontentment was when I told the top crew member to handle a small situation that had developed, and then admonished him for blotching the deal. I realized then that I couldn't take the hands-off approach with them that I was so successful with when running my old crew. After that, I overcompensated by micromanaging everything they did. It all came to a head when their top guy, who was second in line to Amon, arrived late to broker a deal with one of the organization's biggest clients. There were two deals taking place that afternoon, and after one of my many anxiety attacks, I mistakenly mixed up the times. Mustafa was livid about the mix-up because it made him look unprofessional. It didn't help that he felt stepped over when he was bypassed for the head position in a crew that he had played a major part in leading for over ten years. Mr. Walker only put me in the position to give me a first-hand feel of the job he was grooming me for, but Mustafa saw it as a lack of faith in his leadership. He thought it had something to do with his recent squabbles with Amon. Mustafa felt that he was being punished by the very man he blamed for the whole Amon situation. Twice, he had approached Mr. Walker with his concerns about Amon, and both times, he was summarily dismissed.

Mr. Walker Didn't take the mix-up any better than Mustafa; by that time, he had gotten all the information on Amon, so he told Mustafa to take over his operation until they could get Amon back in action. I was relegated back to my small office, scouring through documents and contracts. Mr. Walker realized then that I wasn't the one who could step into his shoes when he would eventually call it quits. I totally agreed with his assessment, I was growing weary of it all. Running my own small crew was a world away from what I was doing now, I spent every day thinking of a way out without embarrassing myself or Mr. Walker. He had put so much time and energy into my criminal education. Even more concerning was the fact that I had amassed so much information on the organization and its operation that I couldn't see them just letting me wander off with enough knowledge to sink the entire ship.

Although Amon was back in shape, and the heat was off from the Dilion murder, he was not allowed to go back into the field. Mustafa ran the crew without incident, but he reported to

Amon by phone whenever anything Major was taking place. Amon spent a lot of time with Dara in the office. The organization was pleased with how she took care of Amon and impressed with how she handled herself during questioning by the cops. Dara was given a position in one of the organization's legitimate subsidiaries. Amon insisted that she never be placed anywhere near any of their shady operations. Mr. Walker agreed.

Mr. Walker was spending a lot of time with Amon; it was clear that he had already replaced me with Amon as his heir apparent. I was pleased with the move, it brought me one step closer to freedom.

One day after a particularly bad anxiety attack, I dredged up enough nerve to tell Mr. Walker how I felt, and he was sympathetic. He suggested that I go back to running my night crew but under the organization's management. We both knew I wasn't cut out for the fast pace I was so unceremoniously pulled into. I was told to report by phone weekly to Amon and him in person monthly. I felt a great sense of relief flow through my body.

CHAPTER FOURTEEN

Back To The Streets

It didn't take me a month to get up to speed with the entire operation of my night crew. As suspected, Terry had everything running like a Swiss watch; she was indispensable. I left her completely in charge and only superseded her decisions when they ran afoul of the organization's guidelines. I gave everyone a big bonus out of my own pocket to go along with the increase they received from the extra business provided by the organization. I even recruited enough people to restart a day crew. They were all locals from the old neighborhood, and I kept them insulated from knowledge of the organization. We eliminated the smash-and-grab operation, expanded the burglaries, and started making drop-off and pick-up services for the organization.

Everything went to shit when one of the guys from the day crew decided to make a few side deals in cocaine and was set up by an undercover Narc. Scared to death of the sentence he was facing, he folded like an old card table and gave up the entire day crew. Thinking back, I could see this coming, it was probably why I kept them in the dark about everything except day crew business. I was the first one picked up by the cops, but I knew better than to open my mouth about anything.

Mr. Walker sent word by a courier that the Organization couldn't provide funds or legal aid without implicating themselves. He knew from my monthly check-in that I had kept the day crew deaf and dumb of the organization's involvement, so none of them were in any position to do it any harm. Mr. Walker also knew that I had limited my contact with both operations and even if any connections were found, it wouldn't be serious enough to warrant a long sentence. Top lawyers expertly handled the money trail so that they wouldn't lead cops to any illegitimate entities. Even the funds that I had amassed were cleverly hidden from scrutiny. The only problem I could foresee was getting enough cash outside of my stash to get decent representation. I had to approach my parents, whom I hadn't spoken to since I left home. I didn't even call when my father had the first of his two heart attacks. I actually sent him a get-well card after the second one. I wasn't exactly a model son. The only thing the cops had on me was knowledge of my meeting with two of the crew members on different occasions. They didn't have audio or video of me saying or doing anything illegal. They charged me with three counts of conspiracy and was hoping that I would crack under pressure. I didn't.

What a farce. Me standing here in my new well-fitted blue suit, clean-shaven, and dawning my bright blue eyes with the kindest, most innocuous expression. My mother was in a sun dress that I had never seen before, with tears in her eyes. I was braced for the worst, despite the sunny disposition of my high-priced lawyer, who was paid for with a second mortgage on a house that my father fully paid off 15 years ago. After much debate, his will was broken by my mother's insistence. It literally killed him to do it. Now we both have to live with the guilt. Despite all of their sacrifices, all I cared about at this point was myself. Who am I kidding, my own safety and well-being were paramount to me above anyone or anything my entire life. I chose a trial by judge over a jury, especially after hearing the sentences handed out to my cohorts. Self-preservation and my smooth-talking lawyer convinced me to separate myself from them in this legal battle. I was portrayed as the good kid led astray by a bad crowd. Little did anyone other than my father know that when it came to criminality, I was the leader of the pack.

www.ingramcontent.com/pod-product-compliance
Lightning Source LLC
LaVergne TN
LVHW090616110826
845146LV00001B/410

* 9 7 9 8 9 8 9 1 6 8 7 1 2 *